SOCCER
SABOTAGE

BY JAKE MADDOX

text by
Eric Stevens

STONE ARCH BOOKS
a capstone imprint

Jake Maddox JV Boys books are published by
Stone Arch Books
a Capstone imprint
1710 Roe Crest Drive
North Mankato, Minnesota 56003

www.mycapstone.com

Cataloging-in-Publication Data is available on the Library of Congress website.
ISBN: 978-1-4965-5932-6 (library binding)
ISBN: 978-1-4965-5934-0 (paperback)
ISBN: 978-1-4965-5936-4 (eBook PDF)

Summary: Jacob, Mohammed, and Simon are the most experienced players on this year's
Narwhals' soccer squad. But during tryouts, a talented newcomer threatens their roles,
which leads to both personal and team conflict.

Designer: Lori Bye

Photo Credits: Shutterstock: Bplanet, chapter openers (design element), Brocreative, 2-3,
(background), sirtravelalot, cover, 1, chapter openers, 95 (background)

Printed and bound in Canada.
010806S18

TABLE OF CONTENTS

CHAPTER 1
SOCCER SEASON **5**

CHAPTER 2
SOCCER HOPEFULS **13**

CHAPTER 3
SECOND-STRING **21**

CHAPTER 4
GETTING PRACTICAL **31**

CHAPTER 5
THE KICKOFF **37**

CHAPTER 6
DIRTY TRICK **45**

CHAPTER 7
SWIRLS OF LAUGHTER **53**

CHAPTER 8
STARTING TO SAG **57**

CHAPTER 9
BREAK A LEG! **65**

CHAPTER 10
DE-CLEATED **71**

CHAPTER 11
NARWHAL ATTACK **79**

CHAPTER 12
RED FLAG **85**

CHAPTER I

SOCCER SEASON

Simon Sanford couldn't stop tapping his pen.

"Mr. Sanford," Ms. Crow hissed. As usual, the Language Arts teacher wore her black hair in a tight bun on top of her head. It seemed to pull her skin tight and stretch her mouth into a smile's evil twin. "There are still three minutes left in the school day."

"I know," Simon said. "I'm paying attention."

"And don't you think everyone else would like to pay attention, too?" Ms. Crow said. "Stop tapping that pen, please!"

"Oh," Simon said. He shoved his pen under his notebook and put his hands in his lap. "Sorry."

He glanced at the clock as Ms. Crow got back to the sonnet on the whiteboard.

Two more minutes, Simon thought. *Two more minutes before it's finally time.*

It was the second week of eighth grade at Northrop Middle School. In two more minutes, the school day would be over. Then it would be time for soccer tryouts.

Simon had been part of the Northrop Narwhals soccer team since sixth grade. But sixth and seventh graders were almost never starters.

In fact, most sixth and seventh graders got zero playing time in games.

But this year, things would be different. This year Simon was in eighth grade. He'd be a starter.

Buzzzzzz!

Simon was out of his seat and halfway to the door before the grating buzzer went quiet again.

He lunged for the classroom door.

"Walking feet, please, Mr. Sanford!" Ms. Crow called after him.

Simon led the rush of students in the hall. Most headed toward their lockers. The odd few who didn't concern themselves with things like books and homework headed straight for the heavy school doors. Someone grabbed Simon's arm.

"Mo!" Simon said.

It was his friend, Mohammed Darr. Mohammed had been on the soccer team with Simon from the beginning, from even before they started school. The two boys went to soccer camp together when they were five.

"You ready for tryouts?" Mohammed asked, slapping Simon's hand. Mohammed was one of the tallest boys in eighth grade. He had big hands and a wide and ready smile.

"Obviously," Simon said.

"You sure?" said another voice.

Simon ducked around Mohammed as they moved through the crowd to find Jacob Klein moving alongside them. Jacob grinned at Simon with narrow eyes. His summer freckles were still dark. His grin was nearly as wicked-looking as Ms. Crow's.

"Hey, Jake," Simon said. "I guess you're heading to tryouts too?"

"Obviously," Jacob said. "Gotta be there to make you look bad, right?"

Although Jacob had been in Simon's life nearly as long as Mohammed, Jacob and Simon were never good friends. It wasn't just because of that wicked smile. Jacob always seemed to get into trouble, and sometimes he'd drag other boys into trouble with him. But Jacob and Mohammed were close friends from way back, so Jacob was usually around — even more during soccer season.

The boys' locker room was already crowded with soccer hopefuls from all grades.

Simon greeted other eighth graders and a few seventh graders he knew from last year. But many of the faces were brand new.

"Wow," Mohammed said. "Big group this year. Lots of competition?"

Simon shook his head. "Doubt it," he said. "Lots of sixth graders, it looks like."

"Works for me," Jacob said. He slapped Simon on the back. "Bunch of babies means *we* get to start."

Rolling his eyes, Simon pulled open his locker. After the boys had changed into their soccer gear, they jogged out to the field.

The day was gray. The trees that towered over the bleachers on one side of the field already boasted leaves of orange, yellow, and red.

The groundskeepers hadn't repainted the lines on the field, so they were still faded from a summer of neglect.

Only the goal nets were new. They were almost as bright and orange as the leaves on the trees.

"Warm-up?" Mohammed said. He used his toe to pry loose a ball from the pile that had tumbled from the open equipment bag near the sideline.

"In a minute," Simon said. "I'm going to go check out the other players."

Simon jogged along the sideline, keeping his eyes on the field, though, to watch the other boys trying out. Most of the new boys weren't great. A few might be good enough to make the team.

One boy Simon didn't recognize juggled a ball by himself in the middle of the field.

Wow, Simon thought. *Impressive.*

The boy caught the ball with the back of his knee and then flicked it over his head. He stalled the ball on the top of his foot, then on the inside of his foot, then on the back of his neck.

But moves like that aren't much help in a real game, Simon thought. *He's just hot-dogging.*

Finally, the boy let the ball drop behind him. He used his heel to pop it up overhead, and then he reared back and slammed it clear across the field and into the goal.

Okay, Simon admitted to himself. *That might be useful in a game.*

"Who is that?" Mohammed said, stepping up next to Simon.

Simon realized he had been standing there gawking at the hot-dogger. He shrugged. "Some sixth grader?" Simon said.

"Nope," said Jacob. He knocked his shoulder against Simon as a tease. "That's Trevor Kraus. He's in eighth."

Simon sneered at Jacob. "What?" he said. "I've never seen that kid before in my life."

"That's because he just moved here. He's in my science class," Jacob said, jogging off while dribbling an orange soccer ball.

"I wouldn't worry about it," Mohammed said. "There's more than one forward position, right?"

"I guess," Simon said.

CHAPTER 2

SOCCER HOPEFULS

Three sharp whistles broke through the noise of the Narwhals soccer hopefuls warming up on the field.

"Good afternoon, gang," said Coach Carter. "Let's bring it on in." He waved the boys over to the bleachers.

Some took a seat. Some stayed on their feet. Simon stood, far too keyed up to sit. He stood near the coach and bounced on his toes. Mohammed stood beside him, stretching his quads.

"Thanks, everyone, for coming out today,"
said Coach Carter. "Many of you have been on
the team a couple of years now. To the rest of you,
welcome. Good luck out there."

He clapped his big, meaty hands a few times.
The older boys knew he wanted everyone to clap
with him, so they did. Soon, the whole gang of
hopefuls was clapping along. A few boys let out
whoops and hollers.

"All right!" Coach Carter said, grinning.
"That's the kind of spirit I want to see this
afternoon. Let's start with some sprints."

The coach had the boys line up at opposite
ends of the field. He explained the drill. They
would first run the length of the field, then sprint
back to the opposite goal box. Then they'd run to
the opposite penalty area, then to the centerline,
and, finally, to the opposite goal box again.

"Got it?" said the coach.

"Yes, Coach!" shouted the older boys.

The sixth graders and Trevor, Simon noticed, stayed silent.

"Let's try that again," Coach Carter said.

He put cupped his hands around his mouth like a megaphone and shouted, "Got it?"

"Yes, Coach!" the whole crew screamed.

Coach clapped once like thunder. "That's better," he said. He blew his whistle sharply.

The boys who were first in line took off. After a few seconds, Coach Carter blasted his whistle again. The next boys started their run.

As Simon moved closer to the front of his line, he saw that Trevor's turn would coincide with his. Sure enough, when Simon reached the front, Trevor stood there facing him on the other end of the field.

Coach Carter blew his whistle.

Simon sprinted toward the other goal.

Trevor crossed the centerline first.

Coming back, Simon pushed harder.

His legs burned. His body seemed to scream in protest. Trevor crossed the centerline even sooner this time. When they passed again, Trevor was way ahead. Trevor finished his turn several seconds before Simon.

When Simon got to the far goal, Mohammed gave him a high five.

Simon, breathless, said, "He beat me."

"So?" Mohammed said. "You were pretty fast."

Simon couldn't answer. He was out of breath, for one thing. But he had to admit to himself that Trevor was a *lot* faster than him.

After the sprints, Coach Carter and two volunteers, sixth graders the coach had picked from the crowd, set up cones.

Simon knew the ball-handling drill well from practices the last two seasons.

The Narwhals hopefuls were to line up at opposite sidelines to take turns. They'd dribble the ball around the cones in a zigzag pattern across the width of the field. After they finished the cones, they'd pass to the boy waiting on the other side of the field. Then they'd get into the back of the line on that side.

Simon whispered to Mohammed behind him. "Trevor's going to kill on this drill," he said.

Jacob, behind Mohammed, leaned forward. He said in a loud voice, "He sure is! Remember his ball-handling skills during warm-up?"

"Yeah, Jake," Simon said. He cringed inside at how loudly Jacob had declared Trevor's skills. "That was my point."

Coach Carter blew his whistle to start the drill.

Simon watched Miguel, another eighth grader he knew from last year's team.

Miguel had decent handling skills, but as he came out of the last cone he overran the ball a little. He stumbled. It was no big deal, really. But it was the kind of mistake Simon would have to avoid if he wanted to stand out against a player like Trevor.

Miguel passed the ball to a sixth grader on the other side of the field. The new boy moved slowly through the cones. Simon could tell, though, that the boy had run a similar drill before. He'd probably make the team, but he wouldn't get a lot of game time.

The boy came out of the cones. Simon was next. He jogged up to take the pass.

The sixth grader passed to Simon, but it went a little wide. Simon recovered quickly, but the bad pass put him off his stride. He entered the cones feeling like he might goof up at any moment.

Simon knew he was moving too slowly. His movements were choppy. He felt off-kilter the whole way through the cones. When he came out of the zigzag, he sighed and looked up at the next player: Trevor Kraus.

Without even thinking, Simon fired the pass to Trevor way too hard. But the new kid handled the rocketing ball with ease. He knocked the pass to the ground with his chest and got it under control in an instant.

Simon watched Trevor have the day's best run on the ball-handling drill.

"Nice try, Simon," Jacob said when he showed up a couple of places behind him in line.

"What?" Simon said, glaring back at Jacob.

"The way you tried to mess up Trevor," Jacob said. "You know, with that wicked pass right at his head."

"Simon wouldn't do that," Mohammed said. "He's not a dirty player."

Simon's teammates' comments caught him off guard. They made him wonder. Maybe he *did* try to mess up Trevor. He hadn't thought about it.

But when it came time to pass to Trevor, was he just grumpy and off his game? Or had he kicked the ball too hard and too high on purpose?

Maybe Jake was right.

CHAPTER 3

SECOND-STRING

After a few more dribbling drills, Coach Carter blew his whistle. He opened the big plastic tub of red pinnies.

"Hopeful future Narwhals!" he shouted. "Line up by height. I want shortest to tallest, starting right in front of me."

The boys hurried to take their places. A sixth grader who could have easily passed for a fourth grader took his spot at the short end of the line in front of Coach Carter.

After some shuffling, the boys lined up pretty much as Coach Carter had asked. Mohammed was way in the back. Simon was stuck somewhere in the middle.

"Count off one-two, one-two," Coach Carter said. He walked alongside the boys, tapping shoulders as he passed.

The boys counted off as Coach Carter tapped them. *One, two, one, two, one, two.*

Simon was a one.

When he reached the back, Coach Carter said, "Twos, put on pinnies. Scrimmage time."

Simon jogged over to Mohammed. He reached him the same time as Jacob. "Ones?" Simon said.

Both other boys nodded. Together, the three boys turned to watch the Twos. They gathered at the tub, pulling pinnies over their heads. Trevor was among them.

"Looks like you get another chance," Jacob said close to Simon's ear.

Simon swiped at his ear like there was a fly in it. "Chance at what?" Simon asked.

"Making Trevor look bad," Jacob said, patting Simon on the back. "Face it. If you can't play better in the scrimmage, your chances of getting a spot as a starting forward are pretty much shot."

"Leave him alone, Jake," Mohammed said, pulling Jacob away.

"Just saying!" Jacob said, grinning like a little kid as Mohammed led them to join the rest of Team One.

Coach Carter had Simon, Mohammed, and Jacob all start for the Ones. A couple of other eighth graders and some of the stronger-looking seventh graders joined them.

Trevor started at right forward for the Twos, directly across the middle line from Simon. When the Twos center started play, he passed to Trevor.

Simon, seeing his chance to outplay the new kid, charged at Trevor to try to steal the ball.

But Trevor's fancy footwork turned out to be tough for Simon. Trevor pulled the ball back away from Simon. Then Trevor spun, toed it up into his own chest, and kneed it in an arc over his head.

When Trevor spun again, he left Simon confused and stumbling. Trevor headed the ball to the ground and took off. He had kept total control of the ball.

Simon gave chase. Luckily, a couple of midfielders stopped Trevor's break. They cleared the ball upfield, where Mohammed got a foot on it.

Trevor jogged back downfield, smiling. "Sorry about that," he said to Simon. "You'll get me next time, right?"

Simon didn't know how to take it. Trevor had almost sounded like he meant it. But maybe he was just teasing Simon, trying to get an edge on him.

Anyway, Simon didn't "get" Trevor the next time. Or the time after that. In fact, Trevor showed Simon up almost every time he got his feet on the ball.

The scrimmage ended with a Twos victory. Trevor scored two goals. Simon had a couple decent plays but never got a decent shot on goal.

"Coach Carter knows you," Mohammed said as he, Simon, and Jacob jogged around the field to warm down with the rest of the hopefuls. "One bad outing doesn't mean much."

"Maybe," Simon said.

As they ran, none of them pushing too hard, Trevor jogged up alongside them.

"Hey," he said. "I'm Trevor. Figured I better get to know the three best veteran players."

"Hi," Jacob replied. He introduced himself, Mohammed, and Simon.

The four boys jogged the last stretch of the warm-down lap in silence. Simon could feel Trevor urging them to quicken the pace.

Jacob, Simon, and Mohammed matched Trevor's speed, but he seemed to move faster and faster. Soon, they weren't really jogging anymore.

They were running hard.

During seventh grade, Mohammed was the fastest player on the team. His long, lean legs gave him a huge advantage. He was also a star on the track team in the spring.

But Trevor seemed to want it more. When they were a hundred yards from the finish, Trevor kicked it into high gear. He easily left Jacob and Simon behind, huffing and puffing and shaking their heads. Mohammed took the bait, and the two boys sprinted for the finish.

"No way he can beat Mo," Simon said to Jacob.

It seemed for a moment that he was right. But then Trevor dug deeper somehow, as if he hadn't even been trying before. He blasted away from Mohammed and took the lead.

Mohammed pumped harder too, his arms and legs like pistons. But it wasn't enough. Trevor crossed the finish line and grinned as he slowed in front of Coach Carter.

When Mohammed caught up, both boys were out of breath. Trevor offered his hand. Mohammed batted it away. Trevor shrugged and walked off.

"That was some warm-down," Coach Carter said, patting Mohammed on the back. "Looks like you've finally got some competition."

As disgusted as Mohammad was with losing to Trevor, Simon was disgusted with Trevor. Why did he need to beat Mo like that, right in front of Coach. It was sort of a cocky thing to do, and Simon thought less of Trevor.

The coach blew his whistle. "Good work out there today, boys," he said. "Go on home. I will post the roster, including the starting lineup, outside my office in the morning."

***

The next day, Simon hurried through the center hallway of Northrop Middle School.

He only had a minute before the buzzer that signaled the beginning of his advisory period.

By the time he reached the athletics office at the back of the school, a number of players and hopefuls were already walking away from the announcements board. A few were grinning and talking, excited to be on the team.

A few hung their heads. It was obvious they had been left off the team roster. If they wanted to play soccer, they'd be stuck on the B team — a collection of sixth and seventh graders who got to play, but just for fun. No real uniforms. No matches against other schools.

Simon wormed through the small crowd to the board and looked up at the list.

"Sorry, man," Mohammed said as he put a hand on his shoulder.

"What?" Simon said, searching for his name.

"Bummer," Jacob said on his other side, shaking his head.

Simon scanned down the starting roster. He saw Mohammed's name. He saw Jacob's name. He saw Trevor's name.

Beneath those, on the list of second-string players, he finally found his.

"I'm not starting," he mumbled, stunned. "I can't believe it."

CHAPTER 4

GETTING PRACTICAL

On Sunday afternoon, Simon, Mohammed, and Jacob went to the park near Simon's house. Though the field wasn't well-kept and the goals had no nets, it was where they'd always practiced. It's even where Simon and Mohammed had gone to soccer camp together when they first met eight summers ago.

"I wouldn't take it lying down, that's all I'm saying," Jacob said. He took his turn at the goal.

Simon shook his head. He walloped a shot toward the upper right corner of the goal.

Jacob jumped and just brushed it with a fingertip. It was enough to send the shot wide.

"I'll get it," Mohammed said. He jogged past the goal to retrieve the stray soccer ball.

Jacob came out of the keeper's box and stopped in front of Simon. "I'm serious," he said.

"About what?" Simon asked.

"About getting rid of Trevor so you can get his spot on the starting lineup," Jacob said.

"Getting rid of him?" Simon said, scoffing. "Are you a magician now?"

Jacob laughed. "Nah," he said. "But a sprained ankle would do the trick."

"You're crazy," Simon said.

"Crazy like a fox," Jacob said, bouncing his eyebrows up and down.

Mohammed jogged up, the ball under his arm. "What foolishness are you talking about now?" he said to Jacob.

"Getting rid of Trevor," Jacob said.

"Sounds good to me," Mohammed said with a shrug. "I don't like being second-fastest."

Simon looked at Mohammed, eyes wide. "Are you really serious?" Simon said. "You think this is a good idea?"

"I'm not saying we should break his kneecaps or anything crazy," Mohammed said. "But I bet we could get him moved to the bench or even off the team completely."

"How?" Simon said.

Jacob sulked a little, grinning. "I don't see why we can't break his kneecaps," he muttered.

Mohammed laughed. "What we need to do is make him miserable," he said. "Ruin his plays. Cleats in the toilet. Uniform on the roof. That kind of thing."

"Those kinds of things would get *us* kicked off the team," Simon pointed out.

"I don't think so," Mohammed said. "They'd be just harmless practical jokes, right?"

"I guess," Simon said, but he wasn't so sure. Usually, it was Jacob's scheming that got people in trouble. But if Mohammed was okay with this kind of thing, maybe it wasn't too bad.

"Fine," Simon finally said, sighing. "But that's where I draw the line: practical jokes. We do nothing that could really get us kicked off the team. Got it?"

Jacob's smile widened till he looked like a hyena. "Or we do whatever it takes and just not get caught," he said.

Simon's heart beat a little faster. His face got hot. He took a deep breath. He knew this kind of behavior was wrong. Jacob being excited about it was a telltale sign.

But what did Simon care about Trevor, anyway? He was just some kid who moved to town and took Simon's rightful spot on the team. Trevor hadn't paid his dues with the Narwhals. He hadn't hauled equipment bags or set up cones or run laps for Coach Carter for the past two years. And he sure didn't warm the bench in sixth and seventh grade like Simon, Mohammed, and Jacob did.

"One more rule," Simon said. "We keep this between us three only. No one else can know what we're up to."

"Obviously," Mohammed said. He put out his hand and looked at his friends expectantly.

Jacob grinned his wicked grin and put his hand on top of Mohammed's.

Though Jacob's sneer gave Simon a shiver, he let the feeling go and put out his hand too. Now, right or wrong, they were committed.

CHAPTER 5

THE KICKOFF

The first official practice for the Northrop Narwhals soccer team was the next day. When Ms. Crow's Language Arts class ended, Simon was almost reluctant to leave the classroom.

As he slowly packed his bag, Ms. Crow sat at her desk. The rest of the class left, and Simon slowly made his way to the door.

"Everything all right, Mr. Sanford?" Ms. Crow said, one narrow eyebrow up.

No, Simon thought. *I'm about to risk getting kicked off the soccer team.*

"I'm fine," he said.

"Don't you have soccer practice to get to?" Ms. Crow said.

"Yes," Simon said.

"You don't seem quite as excited about soccer this afternoon," Ms. Crow pointed out.

"You could say that," Simon admitted. He wanted to say something more to Ms. Crow for some reason. He wanted to tell her about Trevor and about the plan he and Mo and Jacob had come up with. But he knew she would think worse of him for even being associated with such nonsense.

Ms. Crow fixed him with a long stare, swapping raised eyebrows. After a moment, she finally said, "Well, if there's nothing else to say, you'd better get going."

Simon left. His book bag felt especially heavy. His feet were like lumps of lead.

"See you tomorrow," he said.

Ms. Crow smiled. "Goodbye," she said.

After Simon left the classroom, he found Mohammed and Jacob waiting in the hall.

"You ready?" Mohammed said.

Simon took a deep breath and sighed, "Yeah, I guess so. Let's go."

***

"Congratulations, Narwhals," Coach Carter said. He only had to clap a couple of times before the new soccer team caught on and started clapping along. "Welcome to the team."

Simon, standing with Jacob and Mohammed, glanced at Trevor. The new boy stood at the other end of the group of boys. He flashed a smirk as if to say, *Nice try, benchwarmer.*

Simon's face got hot. He set his jaw and kept his eyes on the coach.

Any doubts he had about using foul play to get rid of Trevor vanished.

Coach Carter laid out how practice would go. Laps, drills, and three-on-one shootouts, followed by more laps to close out the session.

The three boys in cahoots stuck together during the warm-up lap around the field.

"So what's the plan?" Jacob said.

"I thought this was Mohammed's plan!" Simon hissed, frowning.

"It was *your* idea," Mohammed said, pointing at Jacob. He gave Jacob a light poke with his elbow.

"It was actually Simon's!" Jacob said. "He's the one who gave the new guy those passes that were tough to handle."

"Yeah, but that wasn't really on purpose," Simon said.

"Oh, come on," said Mohammed.

The boys ran along in silence.

Jacob finally spoke up. "All right," he said. "Let's start simple." He nodded toward Trevor.

Trevor jogged 20 yards or so ahead of them.

"Let's catch up," Jacob said. "Simon, keep an eye on Coach."

"Why?" asked Simon.

"Just do it," Jacob said. "And let me know when he's not watching."

The three friends picked up speed until they were just behind Trevor. Simon glanced over at Coach Carter standing in front of the bleachers on the far side of the pitch. The coach looked right back at him.

"Coach is watching us," said Simon.

"Tell me when he looks away," Jacob said.

Simon kept his eyes on the coach. Though Coach Carter didn't always look right back at Simon, his gaze scanned the field constantly.

"Wait," Simon said, watching the coach.

Coach Carter looked in their direction. Then he pulled the tablet computer from under his arm and tapped the screen.

"Okay," Simon said. "Now!"

Instantly, Jacob kicked out with one foot, knocking Trevor's right foot sideways into his left foot. The kick sent Trevor sprawling onto the grass. Trevor grunted as he hit the turf. Simon had to jump to avoid stepping on him.

"Watch where you're going!" Trevor snapped at the boys. His knees were green from the grass. His face was red with anger.

The three conspirators kept on. They did not offer Trevor a hand or stop to see if he was okay. They finished the lap in front of the coach and began stretching out.

Soon, Trevor finished, glared at the boys, and walked away. Jacob and Mohammed high-fived.

Trevor walked up to he coach.

The coach looked at him. "What's up, Kraus?"

Trevor glanced at Simon, Mohammed, and Jacob, who all quickly looked away. Simon could feel Trevor's eyes on them.

"Yes, Mr. Kraus?" Coach Carter said, loudly.

Trevor finally looked back at the coach.

"Is there something you need?" the coach said.

"No," Trevor said. "Nothing. Never mind."

"Good, because I have a soccer practice to run," Coach Carter said. "Since you're already standing here, you can help get the cones set up."

"Okay, Coach," Trevor muttered. He followed the coach to the equipment bag at the corner of the field.

"He was about to tattle," Jacob said.

"He didn't, though," Mohammed said.

Simon watched Trevor and another couple players set up cones for a ball-handling drill.

Simon knew from how the cones were being placed which drill Coach Carter was about to start.

Trevor probably didn't.

Trevor wasn't really part of this team. That was why the plan to bring him down, Simon reminded himself, was the right thing to do. Trevor would *never* be a part of this team.

CHAPTER 6

DIRTY TRICK

After a few drills, Coach Carter broke the team up into a bunch of three-on-one shootout games. Groups of four were assigned to a goal or a pair of cones. The players took turns defending the goal while the others practiced their shooting skills. Meanwhile, the starting and second-string keepers had their own drills with the assistant coach.

While the coach sorted the players, a few grabbed drinks of water from their bottles on the bleachers.

"Hey, I have an idea," Mohammed said to Simon. "It'll be hilarious."

"What are you gonna do?" Simon asked.

"You'll see," Mohammed said, grinning. Simon had never noticed before that Mohammed's smile could be as nasty as Jacob's.

The boys were split up for the three-on-ones. Simon joined a few of the other benchwarmers at a pair of orange cones set up to be their goal.

"Hey, Simon," said Paul, a seventh grader. "How'd you get stuck with us scrubs?"

Simon rolled his eyes as Coach Carter tossed the four boys a ball so they could start practicing. It would probably be one of the only times Coach would pay attention to the second-stringers all afternoon.

Simon got control of the ball and knocked it to Paul. "I'll keep first," Simon said.

He easily blocked Paul's rolling shot and tossed the ball to the next boy, a sixth grader. That boy's shot on goal was better than Simon would have predicted, but Simon knocked it away easily enough.

Simon spotted Mohammed at one of the actual goals just as his friend flashed a *T* with his hands to take a timeout.

At Simon's second-string drill, the third boy shot. This one sailed over Simon's head. It was a goal. Normally, Simon would have just grabbed the ball and tossed it back into play. But since their "goal" had no net, it flew way out of play and rolled past the benches. It stopped when it bumped into the bleachers.

"Sorry," the shooter said.

"No, it was a good shot," Simon said. He knew, though, that he probably would have blocked it if he hadn't been distracted watching Mohammed. "I'll get it."

He jogged off toward the stray ball and watched as Mohammed took a drink from his own water bottle. Then Mohammed messed with a different bottle near the bleachers before running back to his drill.

Simon used his toe to pop up the ball. He caught it, turned back to his group, and punted it back to them. It was a pretty good kick. "Paul!" he shouted as he ran back. "Your turn to keep!"

The drills ran most of the afternoon. Simon found himself enjoying practicing with the three other benchwarmers enough to forget his struggles. These boys seemed to actually be having fun. Simon thought about that. It struck him that this was a very different experience than playing with Mohammed and Jacob lately. They were always so competitive.

Coach Carter blew his whistle. "Bring it in, Narwhals!" he shouted across the field.

As Simon and Paul jogged in with the rest of the team, Simon found himself smiling. Then he spotted Trevor hurrying toward him and dribbling the soccer ball. Simon's smile vanished.

"Looking good out there, everyone," Coach Carter said. "Have some water. Stay hydrated."

The boys found their water bottles on the benches and bleachers. Simon took a long drink and then sprayed some water over his head. Mohammed came up next to him. Jacob walked up on the other side.

"Check this out," Mohammed said, nodding toward Trevor a few yards away.

Simon watched as Trevor pulled open the top of his water bottle. He held it upside down over his wide-open mouth. He closed his eyes, prepared for ice-cold refreshment, and squeezed.

Thick, brown mud squirted all over his face and into his mouth.

Trevor gagged and shouted. He tossed his water bottle to the grass. He coughed and spit. He did his best to wipe mud from his face.

Simon, Mohammed, and Jacob struggled to keep from laughing. But then a few other Narwhals started cracking up. Finally, the three troublemakers couldn't hold it in any longer.

"Who did that?" Trevor shouted. He spit again and jerked his stare from this player to that one. The wild look on his dirty face just made everyone laugh even more.

"All right, all right," Coach Carter said over the laughter. He blew his whistle, shrill and long.

Everyone stopped laughing.

"Trevor, hit the showers," said the coach. "The rest of you, take a warm-down lap."

Trevor picked up his mud-filled water bottle and twisted off the top as he stomped off toward the locker room. He dumped the mud as he went, leaving a trail behind him. Some splattered on his socks.

When he was out of earshot, Simon, Mohammed, and Jacob started laughing again.

"Something extra funny to you?" Coach Carter said, stepping up to them and crossing his arms.

"No, Coach," Jacob said.

Simon shook his head.

Mohammed looked at the clouds.

Coach Carter stood there. He glared at the boys for a long moment. "Why don't you three actually take two laps," he said. "Then hit the showers."

The three boys started their laps. Simon looked back to see Trevor walking toward the school's back doors. Trevor walked slowly now, his shoulders slumped.

"How'd Coach know it was us?" Jacob wondered aloud.

Mohammed shook his head, stumped.

"Doesn't matter," Simon said. "It was worth it."

CHAPTER 7

SWIRLS OF LAUGHTER

The next day, Mohammed, Jacob, and Simon got to the locker room a few minutes before the rest of the team. When they'd all changed into their uniforms, Jacob opened someone else's locker.

"Looks like someone hasn't got a padlock yet," Jacob said, grinning. He pointed at a strip of masking tape inside the door: *T. Kraus.*

"How'd you know that's his locker?" Simon said.

"You said you wanted a plan," Jacob said. "So I've been planning." He reached in and grabbed Trevor's practice gear and said, "Gross. He didn't bring it home to wash after he got it all muddy."

"He got it all muddy?" Mohammed said. "Don't I get any credit?"

Simon and Jacob laughed.

"Hide it or something," Simon said.

"So he'll be late to practice," Mohammed said. "Coach Carter hates that. A couple of tardies, and Trevor will be off the team."

"Nah," Jacob said. "I'm gonna wash it for him."

Simon looked at Mohammed, who shrugged.

Jacob carried Trevor's gear to the bathroom. He looked around and scratched his chin.

"What are you doing?" Simon said.

Suddenly, an *aha!* expression spread across Jacob's face. He headed into a stall.

"Oh no," Mohammed said, giggling. "No way."

Simon and Mohammed stood in the stall doorway and watched as Jacob dipped Trevor's practice shorts and jersey into the toilet. He flushed but hung on to the gear as the water rushed and tugged at the clothing.

The bowl roared and the water swirled, twirling the red and gold gear into a whirlpool. The water rose, nearly overflowing, until it finally stopped. Trevor's clothes floated at the top, twisted. The dry mud seeped into the water, making the toilet look especially gruesome.

"There we go," Jacob said, wiping his hands. "We should probably let it soak, now. Tough stain he's got, there."

Simon couldn't believe it. What a guilty thrill it was to see Trevor's clothes in the toilet.

The boys laughed themselves silly as they left the bathroom.

Soon, the rest of the team arrived. Trevor opened his locker and stood there staring at the emptiness for a long moment. Briefly, he caught the three culprits' gaze for an awkward moment.

Simon said, "Let's go," and the three friends hurried out of the locker room and onto the field.

CHAPTER 8

STARTING TO SAG

The Narwhals were doing stretches when Trevor finally showed up on the field for practice. He was wearing baggy yellow sweatpants and a T-shirt that read: *River City Tractor Expo 2003*.

"Wow, Trevor," Jacob called over the heads of the other players. "Where'd you dig up that outfit?"

A few teammates laughed.

"Pretty sure that's not regulation," Simon said, though not as loudly as Jacob.

This got a laugh from Mohammed and Jacob. Trevor's face turned red. He turned and stared darkly at Simon.

If Coach Carter noticed the friction between the boys, he didn't acknowledge it. "Okay," he said. "Time to take your warm-up jog."

The boys took off. The afternoon was hot for September. Before they finished a lap, Simon's forehead and back dampened with sweat. Trevor slogged along in heavy sweatpants, surely hotter than anyone else on the team.

When finished running, the team gathered to listen to Coach Carter go over a few of the familiar drills. It was all stuff that Simon and his friends were familiar with from their last two years on the team.

"Jacob and Mohammed," Coach Carter said. "Come out and show the rest of the team this drill."

Simon's friends headed out. Jacob positioned himself on one side of a four-cone "wall" with Mohammed on the other. Coach Carter tossed a bright orange ball, and Mohammed knocked it down with his knee.

Mohammed and Jacob each darted back and forth on their side of the cones, deftly passing the ball between the gaps as they did. They moved quickly and kept the ball in motion the whole time.

They'd probably done this drill together a hundred times. Simon smiled, feeling a little pride for his friends. Then he remembered they were starting, and he was not.

"Thank you," Coach Carter said. "Keep it up. The rest of you, partner up. Take a ball, and start drilling with the rest of the cones."

Simon partnered up with Paul, the same seventh grader he'd worked with before. They headed to a series of cones on the far side of the field. Paul took a few tries to get the hang of the drill, and more than once they had to stop to fix the cones. It didn't help Simon's mood that Trevor was at the neighboring set of cones with Kyle, another starter. They caught on to the drill easily.

Simon got back into position after fixing a couple of cones. "Ready?" he asked.

Paul nodded.

Simon passed, and Paul knocked it right back through the next set. Simon shuffled to his right, stopped the pass, and kicked it back to Paul. It was a good pass, but Paul didn't get in front of it.

"Sorry," Paul said. "My bad. I'll get it."

As Paul jogged off to retrieve the stray ball, Simon watched Kyle and Trevor. Trevor's sweatpants were too big. He had to hold the waist to keep them from falling down as he ran.

"Ready?" Paul called. He heaved the ball like a throw-in.

Simon stopped it with his chest, juggled it a second, and started the drill again. The two boys got a good rally going, each completing a dozen or so good passes.

Coach Carter walked among the players as they drilled, sometimes shouting corrections and sometimes shouting encouragement. "Nice going, guys," he said as he passed behind Simon. "I'm happy to see you performing up to your ability, Mr. Sanford."

"Thanks, Coach," Simon said. But the compliment stung. It didn't just mean he was playing well today. It meant he hadn't been playing well before today.

When Coach Carter moved on, Simon's heart sank a little. He fudged a pass, which knocked a cone and rolled out of play.

"Sorry," Simon said.

"No problem," Paul said, already jogging after the stray ball.

Simon watched Trevor and Kyle again. Kyle knocked a fast pass toward Trevor. It just caught a cone's edge, sending it a bit off course.

It was enough, though, to throw Trevor off. He quickly cut to his right to recover, but as he did, he let go of the waistband of his sweatpants.

The pants dropped to his ankles, tripping him. He fell to the grass with his pants down.

Everyone laughed, even Coach Carter. But maybe no one laughed louder than Simon.

Trevor got to his feet and tugged up his sweatpants. He immediately looked at Simon.

Simon couldn't stop laughing. When Trevor clenched his jaw and snarled like a bull about to charge, Simon just laughed more.

That was it for Trevor. The new boy charged at Simon, caught him around the middle, and knocked him to the ground.

They scrapped for only a moment before Coach Carter pulled Trevor off. Paul grabbed Simon's arms too, to hold him back.

"Kraus," Coach Carter said, struggling to hold the boy back. "Hit the showers. Go cool off."

Trevor started to protest.

"I said cool off!" Coach Carter ordered. He let go of Trevor's arms. "I don't like hot tempers."

Trevor stumbled forward, tugged up his pants a little more, and stalked across the field to the locker room.

"I don't have a partner now, Coach," Kyle said.

Coach Carter looked at Simon. "You partner with Kyle," he said. "I'll drill with you, Paul."

"Me, Coach?" Simon said.

"You're a better match with Kyle than with Paul," Coach Carter said. He blew his whistle. "Now get back to work. No reason to stand around gawking like a bunch of slack-jawed bumpkins."

Simon jogged to the cones Trevor had been using with Kyle.

"Ready?" Kyle said.

Simon nodded and glanced past Kyle toward the school's back doors. There was Trevor, sulking and sagging as he went back inside. It was now the second time that Trevor had been sent to the shower before practice was finished.

CHAPTER 9

BREAK A LEG!

Trevor started bringing his uniform home every day. Then he showed up with a new water bottle that clearly showed its contents. But for the next week of practices, Simon, Mohammed, and Jacob continued to make life difficult for Trevor.

Simon began to feel more and more guilty by the day. At the same time, though, he was frustrated. Why wouldn't Trevor just give up and quit? Who'd want to stay on a team with people who obviously don't want him around?

The following Tuesday would be the season's first game. It was an away game the next town over.

On Tuesday afternoon, when Ms. Crow's class ended, Simon lingered at his desk.

"First game today, isn't it Mr. Sanford?" Ms. Crow said.

"Yeah," Simon said. He carefully put his four-color pen into its sleeve in the smallest pocket of his bag.

She walked over, sat at the desk in front of Simon's, and swiveled to talk to him. "You're not enjoying being on the team as much this year, are you?" she said.

Simon shrugged. Why was Ms. Crow so concerned about Simon's happiness on the team? "I guess not," he said.

"As I recall," Ms. Crow said, "on tryouts day you could hardly stay in your seat."

Simon didn't reply.

"Didn't you get the position you wanted?" Ms. Crow said.

"Not exactly," Simon said.

"That must be very disappointing," Ms. Crow said. "Did you know I was an actor when I lived in New York?"

Simon didn't even know she'd lived in New York. He shook his head.

"Well, I was," she went on. "My dearest dream my whole life was to act on Broadway. I studied drama in college. And before that, I had the starring role in nearly every high school play and musical."

Simon tried to imagine it. His stiff and stern Language Arts teacher standing on a stage? Wearing a costume, acting, and maybe even singing for an audience? Simon simply could not produce a mental image. "What happened then?" he asked.

"Well, I auditioned for show after show," Ms. Crow said. "Now and then, I even got a small part."

"That's good," Simon said.

"Well," said Ms. Crow, "it wasn't good enough for me. I didn't want minor roles. I didn't want to be a chorus member or a secondary character in some off-off-Broadway show. I didn't want to be some star's understudy. I wanted to be a star. I wanted to be *the* star."

"I can sure understand that," Simon said.

Ms. Crow smiled. It wasn't her normal smile, the one that made a chill run up Simon's back. It was softer and kinder.

"So do you know what I did?" Ms. Crow asked.

"Did you try to get the star fired so you could take over the role?" Simon asked.

Ms. Crow laughed. "No," she said. "I gave up. I came back here, got my teaching license, and got a job at Northrop."

"Oh," Simon said. "Not a very happy ending."

Ms. Crow shrugged. "I wouldn't say that," she said. "I like my life. I like teaching, and I love directing the drama club every spring. But still . . . "

"You wonder what would've happened if you'd stayed in New York and kept trying?" Simon said.

"No," Ms. Crow said. "I think that maybe I could have been happy as a chorus member or as a secondary character."

"Or an understudy," Simon put in.

"Right," Ms. Crow said. "Because I really loved the stage. I love drama. I love musicals. And that means being a part of something larger than just yourself. It means teamwork."

Simon waited for her to go on, but she didn't. She patted his hand, stood up, and headed back to her desk. "I'll need to lock up in a minute, Mr. Sanford," she said with her back to him.

"Okay," Simon said. "Thanks, Ms. Crow."

She smiled and said, "Break a leg!"

A twinge of fear struck Simon. Ms. Crow knew what he and Mo and Jacob were up to! Then Simon realized that Ms. Crow was just talking in drama language, and the twinge went away.

CHAPTER 10

DE-CLEATED

Simon, Mohammed, and Jacob took up the whole back row of the bus. Their gear sat in duffel bags under their seats. Simon stared out the window as they rolled down Route 8 past fast-food restaurants, gas stations, and strip malls.

"Hey," Mohammed said. "Cheer up."

"Why?" Simon said. "I'll probably get like two minutes of playing time today."

"Yeah, the last two minutes," Mohammed said, laughing. "And only if we're winning."

Jacob smirked. "I don't know," he said. "I have a feeling you'll be starting today instead of Trevor."

"What are you talking about?" Simon said.

Jacob leaned in closer. He whispered, "Let's just say Trevor should have double-checked his duffel bag before we got on the bus."

"Huh?" Simon said.

"He *forgot* his gear," Jacob said, putting up air quotes. "No cleats, no shin guards, no water bottle. All he's got in his bag are a few rolls of toilet paper I found in the locker room's storage closet. Oh, and one of my little sister's dolls."

Mohammed's eyes went wide.

Simon's stomach flipped. His heart jumped into his throat. "Where did you put his stuff?" he asked.

"It's fine," Jacob said. "I just shoved it into the back of my locker. You know what a mess it is in there."

"You should not have done that," Simon said. "For one thing, if you get caught, you'll get in serious trouble."

Mohammed nodded. "Off the team for sure," he said.

"Probably worse," Simon says. "And I said we stick to pranks. Harmless stuff, not stuff that will get us kicked off the team."

"No one's getting kicked off the team," Jacob said, "because no one's getting caught." He sat back in his seat and crossed his arms, smirking.

"Not to mention that Trevor's actually a *good* player," Simon said.

"So?" Jacob said.

"So," Simon said, "I want to win the game, too, not just be a starter."

"Should've thought of that before we started this plan," Jacob pointed out.

"I guess I should have," Simon said. "I'm thinking it now."

Jacob shrugged. "Too late, now," he said.

The Northrop bus pulled into the circle at Franklin Middle School. Simon looked out at the school. The big, modern school was nothing like Northrop, which was musty and old fashioned-looking.

The team piled off the bus, one-by-one. Each player gripped his duffel or carried it slung over one shoulder.

Simon, who climbed down last, spotted Trevor at the head of the pack. Since he'd managed to dodge the pranksters' tricks the last few practices, he'd been in a better mood.

Simon knew it wouldn't last.

The team dropped their gear at the visitors' bench. Bags unzipped. Boys wearing warm-up pants or hoodies over their uniforms peeled off the layer to get ready for the game. Velcro grabbed and ripped, too, as the players strapped on shin guards.

Coach Carter paced behind the bench. He and the assistant looked at their tablets, going over the roster.

Only Trevor wasn't getting ready for the game. He kneeled at the end of the bench opposite Simon, digging through his bag as if the missing items would finally appear. He pulled out a few rolls of toilet paper. He pulled out a doll with long, pink hair. He stood up and threw the doll to the ground.

Jacob laughed as he strode over to Trevor. "Hey, Trevor," Jacob said, sneering. "Why did you bring your dolly?" He winked at Simon.

Trevor just glared back at him. Then he headed toward Coach Carter.

"You can't prove a thing," Jacob said under his breath as Trevor walked past.

Simon got up from the bench and hurried toward the coach and Trevor.

As he got there, Trevor addressed the coach. "Coach," he said, "I can't play today."

"What?" Coach Carter said. "Why not?"

"Yes, he can," Simon said, taking Trevor by the arm. "He's just nervous."

Simon pulled Trevor aside. Coach Carter narrowed his eyes but stepped away.

"What are you doing?" Trevor said, yanking his arm out of Simon's grasp.

"Stopping you from giving up," Simon said. "It's my fault."

Trevor shook his head. "I know it was Jacob who took my stuff," he said.

"But he did it for me," Simon said. He took a deep breath and said, "He did it because you took my starting spot. At first I was on board with it, but now I've changed my mind. So I'm going to let you use my gear today. It should fit you."

Trevor looked hard at Simon.

"I'm sorry," Simon said. He crouched to untie his cleats and pull off his shin guards. He stood up and handed them to Trevor.

"Fine," Trevor said, taking off his sneakers. "I'll accept your help and your gear." He pulled on the cleats and strapped on the shin guards. "But I won't accept your apology," he said, standing up.

Trevor ran onto the field wearing Simon's cleats. That's when it sunk in to Simon that he wouldn't be playing. You can't play without wearing your cleats. He thought of all the mistakes he'd made that had put him in the position of being "de-cleated."

Jacob came up behind Simon. "Hey," he said.

When Simon turned, Jacob shoved him.

"Why'd you do that?" Jacob said.

"Because this has gotten out of hand," Simon said. "I was jealous. Now I'm over it."

Mohammed stepped between them to prevent any further clash. Jacob shook his head and jogged onto the field.

CHAPTER 11

NARWHAL ATTACK

It was a tight match. The Franklin Foxes had a hard-nosed defense. During the first half, neither team scored.

The Foxes stayed on their heels under constant pressure from the Narwhals' offense — led by Trevor. Still, the Narwhals' every strike was thwarted by the Foxes.

Trevor drove hard up the right side. The Foxes cut him off and flanked him hard. He passed to Mohammed, but the Foxes intercepted and cleared the ball.

On the next drive, Jacob got open on the left.
He took the ball up to the defense. Mohammed cut
across the pitch, but he couldn't get open.

Jacob's drive stalled. A Fox defender nabbed
the ball and punted it back across midfield.

At halftime Coach Carter tried to motivate his
team. "We've had our chances," he said. "We just
need to take better advantage of them. Don't give
up. Keep attacking."

Simon handed Trevor his water bottle.

"It's clean," Simon said. "I swear."

Trevor took a drink.

"What I'd like to see," the coach continued, "is
some better coordination on those strikes."

Jacob sat on the bench next to Simon.

"Jacob Klein," Coach Carter said, "and Trevor
Kraus. You two are our most aggressive players,
but you're not working together."

Trevor and Jacob leaned forward to glance at
each other around Simon.

"We've worked on this in practice," Coach Carter said, pacing in front of the three boys on the bench. "We've drilled it. We've gone over it. Now we need to use it."

"Okay, Coach," said Trevor.

Jacob stayed silent.

"We're wearing them down," Coach Carter said. "Show us what the two of you can do together, and we'll have this game in the bag."

***

When the second half started, the play was much like the first half. For the Narwhals, Jacob and Trevor moved the ball upfield, keeping constant pressure on the Fox defense.

With only a few minutes left in the half, the Fox defense cleared another Narwhal attack. This time, though, the ball sailed off the field and well out of bounds.

Simon grabbed it and tossed it to the ref.

It felt good to have his hands on the ball, even just for a moment.

Jacob jogged over for the throw-in.

"Jake," Simon called to him before he launched the ball back into play. "You and Trevor are going to have to connect!"

Jacob looked back at Simon. His eyes narrowed. Then he turned back to the field, raised the ball over his head, and heaved it into play.

Mohammed took the throw-in. He faked right, rolled left, and took a few steps before passing to Trevor in the middle.

Trevor broke fast toward the goal. Jacob ran along the right sideline, found an opening, and crossed the middle.

Trevor passed. Jacob picked it up and faked to his right. Then he passed back to Trevor as Trevor moved across the top of the penalty arc.

"Shoot!" Jacob shouted.

Trevor was already drawing back for the shot. He faked right and fired a perfect shot into the top left corner as the goalkeeper dove the other way.

Goal!

Trevor and Mohammed jumped and high-fived. Simon leaped up from the bench, cheering along with the rest of the second stringers.

Jacob glared, stone-faced. He jogged to the centerline for the kickoff.

The Foxes restarted play. But the game was nearly over. The seconds on the clock wound down until the referee blew the final whistle. The Narwhals had won their first game!

As the teams slapped hands and exchanged *good games*, only Jacob sulked.

RED FLAG

The next afternoon, Simon walked into Ms. Crow's class. He felt better about the soccer team. Last week he almost dreaded practice and the looming first game. Now, though, he looked forward to practice and games.

"Mr. Sanford," Ms. Crow said. "I'm to send you to Mr. Carter's office."

"*Coach* Carter?" Simon asked. "Why?"

Ms. Crow clasped her hands and threw back her shoulders. For the first time, Simon could see how she might have been a great actor.

With her chin high, she said, *"Theirs not to reason why . . ."*

"Is that from some play?" Simon said.

Ms. Crow frowned at him. "I see we have some work to do on last week's reading assignment," she said.

"Oh," Simon said. "Oops."

"Oops, indeed," Ms. Crow said, shaking her head. "Now get going."

Simon grabbed his book bag and hopped out of his seat. Out in the hallway, he knocked into Mohammed, nearly toppling the both of them.

"You too, huh?" Mohammed said.

"You know what this is about?" Simon asked.

"I have a pretty good guess," Jacob said as he jogged up behind them.

Simon looked up and down the hallway as they walked. Except for the three of them, it was empty.

When they reached Coach Carter's office, they found him sitting behind his barren metal desk.

"I think it's about time you three told me what's been going on," the coach said.

The boys glanced at each other quickly and then looked at the floor.

"Well?" the coach said.

Simon took a deep breath. There was no point in keeping this from the coach anymore. "It's my fault, Coach," Simon said. He kept his eyes on the floor.

The coach sighed. "*What* is your fault?" he said.

Simon glanced at his friends. "I was upset you didn't make me a starter," Simon said. He finally looked the coach in the eye.

"So you blamed Trevor Kraus," the coach said.

Simon nodded.

"That explains the pranks," Coach Carter said. He stood behind his desk and began to pace. "But stealing his equipment? And on game day?"

"Trevor told you?" Jacob said, his eyes wide.

"I got the info out of him," said Coach Carter. "But he wouldn't give up a name."

"So why'd you call us here?" Mohammed asked.

"I had a hunch," said Coach Carter. "And Jacob just confirmed it. You three could be in big trouble."

The boys sat silent once again.

Jacob took a quick, angry breath through his nose. "I did it," he said through his teeth. "Just me."

"But he did it *for* me," Simon put in. "So I'd be able to start since Trevor couldn't play without gear."

The coach stopped pacing. He leaned his big hands on the desktop and stared at Jacob. "You crossed a line," Coach Carter said.

"I know," Jacob said quietly.

"Trevor could let the police know," the coach said. "Those cleats aren't cheap."

"I'll give them back," Jacob protested.

"You sure will!" the coach said. "I hope they're someplace safe and not in a dirty toilet this time."

He sighed and sat down again. "I'm looking for a good reason not to throw the three of you off the team," he said.

"Off the team?" Mohammed said. "Oh man, my mom would kill me if I got thrown off the team."

Simon took a deep breath, but he stayed quiet. He realized how much soccer meant to him in that moment, but he didn't know what to say.

"They knew about some of the pranks," Jacob said, rising from his chair. "They were even in favor of some of them. But I pulled the pranks. I messed with Trevor's uniform, his water bottle, and everything else. I should get punished, not them."

The coach looked up at Jacob. "You sure about that, Jacob?" he asked. "You accept all the blame?"

Jacob nodded.

Coach nodded back. "Bring your uniform in," he said. "Maybe I'll see you for baseball in the spring."

Jacob looked at his friends, turned, and left.

The buzzer to end last period sounded.

"Go get changed for practice," the coach said.

Simon and Mohammed hurried to the locker room. They found Jacob sulking in front of his locker.

"Thanks," Simon said.

Jacob just reached into his locker and pulled out his uniform. He dropped it on the bench.

"Yeah," Mohammed added, "Thanks."

Jacob dumped the rest of the stuff in his locker into his book bag. He slung his bag over his shoulder and shoved his way past both of them.

Mohammed sighed and said, "He'll get over it."

"Maybe," Simon said, but he couldn't help thinking the whole thing was his fault.

Fifteen minutes later, Simon and Mohammed were first out to the field for practice. They jogged right onto the track for a warm-up lap.

"Hey!" someone called from behind.

Simon looked over his shoulder. Trevor sprinted to catch up with them. "Can I run with you?" he said.

"Why?" Mohammed asked.

"I decided to let it all go," Trevor said.

The boys regarded each other for a moment.

"Thanks," Mohammed finally said.

"Sure," Trevor said. "And I'm going to talk to Coach Carter about getting Jacob back on the team."

"It won't work," Simon said.

"It might," Trevor said.

"It won't," Mohammed said. "You might be the best player on the team. But we know Coach better than you. He won't change his mind about this."

"Maybe that's true," Trevor admitted. "The first part anyway, about me being the best on the team."

Simon gave Trevor a shove. They all laughed.

"Teammates?" Trevor said.

Mohammed nodded.

Trevor looked at Simon. "Even if the coach doesn't make you a starter," he said, "there's no shame in being the back-up to a great player."

Simon sprinted up ahead and called back, "You better speed up."

Trevor and Mohammed turned it up a notch. They didn't catch Simon until the very last moment.

Eric Stevens has written more than one hundred chapter books for young readers. He lives with his wife and children in Minneapolis, where he and his family enjoy kayaking, cycling, and playing tennis in the city's beautiful parks.

GLOSSARY

benchwarmer (BENCH-wahr-mur)—a reserve player on a team; a player who sits on the bench

hotdogging (HAHT-dawg-ing)—to perform fancy stunts or maneuvers; to show off

megaphone (MEG-ah-fohn)—a cone-shaped device used to make a voice louder

midfielder (MID-feel-duhr)—a soccer player who plays most often in the central part of the field

pinnies (PIN-ees)—a colored jersey, often made of mesh material, used for differentiating teams in a sports practice setting

sabotage (SAB-uh-taj)—to damage, destroy, or interfere with on purpose

second-string (SEK-uhn STRING)—the players who are available to replace those who start the game

showboating (SHOW-boht-ing)—trying to attract attention by showing off or acting conspicuously

throw in (THROW IN)—in soccer, a method of restarting play when the ball has gone out of bounds on the sideline

DISCUSSION QUESTIONS

1. Simon was very excited for the start of soccer season, but his excitement quickly waned. Why did his enthusiasm fade? Has this ever happened to you?

2. Discuss Simon's friendship with Jacob. Do the boys seem like good friends?

3. Simon's priorities when it comes to soccer change over the course of the story. What caused the change in his feelings? Use examples from the story.

WRITING PROMPTS

1. Simon went along with Jacob's plan to get Trevor kicked off the team even though he knew it wasn't a very good idea. Write about a time you went along with your friends when perhaps you shouldn't have.

2. Write the scene where Trevor discovers his uniform in the toilet from Trevor's point of view.

3. Simon begins to see Ms. Crow in a new light as the story progresses. Write a short essay about a time you changed your mind about an authority figure.

MORE ABOUT SOCCER

There are often three forwards on a team. Forwards play closest to the opponent's goal and are the most likely to score. A forward can also be called a striker, but sometimes the term is used to refer to the forward that is the main scorer.

Juggling the soccer ball and doing tricks is known as freestyle soccer or freestyle football. Competitions are held all over the world every year, where players perform tricks such as "Crossover," "Toe Bounce," and "Around the World."

Though soccer is popular all over the world, the earliest known version of the game was played as a military exercise in China — over two thousand years ago.